Samuel Rowlands

Humors Looking Glasse

Samuel Rowlands

Humors Looking Glasse

ISBN/EAN: 9783337364786

Printed in Europe, USA, Canada, Australia, Japan

Cover: Foto ©Andreas Hilbeck / pixelio.de

More available books at **www.hansebooks.com**

Hunterian Club

No. II.—1871-2.

HUMORS

LOOKING GLASSE

BY
SAMUEL ROWLANDS

REPRINTED FROM THE FIRST EDITION
1608

PRINTED FOR THE HUNTERIAN CLUB
1872

HUMORS
LOOKING
Glasse.

LONDON.
Imprinted by *Ed. Allde* for *William Fere-*
brand and are to be sold at his Shop in
the popes-head Pallace, right over a-
gainst the Taverne-dore.
1608.

To his verie Loving Friend Master George Lee.

Esteemed friend, I pray thee take it kinde,
That outward action beares an inward minde,
What objects heere these papers do deliver,
Bestow the viewing of them for the giver.
I make thee a partaker of strange sights,
Drawne antique works of humours vaine delights.
A mirrour of the mad conceited shapes,
Of this our ages giddy-headed apes,
These fash'on mongers, selfe besotted men
Of kindred to the fowle that wore my pen,
Are at an howers warning to appeare,
And muster in sixe sheetes of Paper heere.
And this is all at this time I bestow,
To evidence a greater love I owe.

Yours SAMUEL ROWLANDS.

Reader.

As many antique faces passe,
From Barbers chaire unto his glasse,
There to beholde their kinde of trim,
And how they are reform'd by him,
Or at *Exchang* where Marchants greete,
Confusion of the tongues do meete,
As *English, French, Italian, Dutch,*
Spanish, and *Scot'sh,* with divers such.
So from the Presse these papers come
To show the humorous shapes of some.
Heere are such faces good and bad,
As in a Barbers shop are had,
And heere are tongues of divers kindes,
According to the speakers mindes.
Beholde their fashions, heare their voice,
And let discretion make thy choice.

SAMUELL ROWLANDS.

Epigram.

Some man that to contention is inclin'de;
With any thing he sees, a fault wil finde,
As, that is not so good, the same's amisse,
I have no great affection unto this.
Now I protest I doe not like the same,
This must be mended, that deserveth blame,
It were farre better such a thing were out,
This is obscure, and that's as full of doubt.
And much adoe, and many words are spent
In finding out the path that humours went,
And for direction to that Idle way
Onely a busie tongue bears all the sway.
The dish that *Aesope* did commend for best;
Is now a daies in wonderfull request,
But if you finde fault on a certaine ground,
Weele fall to mending when the fault is found.

Epigram.

Pra'y by your leave, make moūsieur humors roome
That oft hath walk'd about Duke Humphries tombe
And sat amongst the Knights to see a play,
And gone in's suite of Sattin ev'ry day,
And had his hat display a bushie plume,
And's verie beard deliver forth perfume.
But when was this? aske Frier Bacons head
That answered *Time is past*, O time is fled!
Sattin and silke was pawned long agoe,
And now in canvase, no knight can him knowe.
His former state, in dark oblivion sleepes,
Onely Paules Gallarie, that walke he keepes.

Epigram.

Crosse not my humor, with an ill plac'd worde,
For if thou doest, behold my fatall sworde:
Do'st see my countenance begin looke red?
Let that fore-tell ther's furie in my hed.
A little discontent will quickely heate it.
Touch not my stake, thou wert as good to eate it,
These damned dice how cursed they devoure:
I lost some halfe score pound in halfe an houre.
A bowle of wine, sirha: you villaine, fill:
Who drawes it Rascall? call me hether *Will*.
You Rogue, what ha'st to Supper for my dyet?
Tel'st me of Butchers meate? knave I defie it.
Ile have a banquet to envite an Earle,
A *Phœnix* boyld in broth distil'd in Pearle.
Holde drie this leafe, a candle quickly bring,
Ile take one pipe to bed, none other thing.
Thus with *Tabacco* he will sup to night:
Flesh-meate is heavie, and his purse is light.

Epigram.

Two Gentlemen of hot and fierie sprite,
Tooke boate, and went up Westward to goe fight
Imbarked both, for Wens-worth they set saile,
And there ariving with a happie gaile,
The Water-men discharged for their fare,
Then to be parted, thus their mindes declare.
Pray Ores (said they) stay heere and come not nie,
We goe to fight a little, but heere by.
The Water-men with staves did follow then,
And cryd, oh holde your hands good Gentlemen,
You know the danger of the law, forbeare:
So they put weapons up and fell to sweare.

Epigram.

One of these Cuccold-making Queanes
did graft her husbands head:
who arm'd with anger, steele and horne
would kill him stain'd his bed,
And challeng'd him unto the field,
Vowing to have his life,
Where being met, sirha (quoth he,)
I doe suspect my Wife
Is scarce so honest as she should,
You make of her some use:
Indeed said he I love her well,
Ile frame no false excuse.
O! d'ye confesse? by heavens (quoth he)
Had'st thou deni'de thy guilt,
This blade had gone into thy guts,
Even to the verie Hilt.

Epigram.

Occasion late was ministred for one to trie his friend,
Ten pounds he did intreat him yᵗ of all love he would lēd
His case was an accursed case, no comfort to be found,
Unles he friendly drew his purse, & blest him with tē poūd
He did protest he had it not, making a solemne vow,
He wāted means & money both, to do him pleasure now.
Thē sir (quoth he) you know I have a Gelding I love wel,
Necessitie it hath no law, I must my Gelding sell,
I have bin offered twelve for him, with ten ile be cōtent,
Well I will trie a friend (said he,) it was his chest he ment.
So fectch'd the money presently, tother sees Angels shine
Now God amercy horse (quoth he) thy credit's more then
      mine.

Epigram.

Dice diving deepe into a Ruffians purse,
Leaving it nothing worth but strings and leather:
He presently did fall to sweare and curse,
That's life and money he would loose together,
Tooke of his hat, and swore, let me but see
What Rogue dares say this same is blacke to me?

Another lost, and he did money lacke,
And thus his furie in a heate revives:
Where is that Rogue denies his hat is blacke?
Ile fight with him, had he ten thousand lives.
Oh sir (quoth he) in troth you come too late,
Choller is past, my anger's out of date.

Epigram.

A Kinde of *London*-walker in a boote,
(Not *George* a Horse-backe, but a *Gerge* a foote,)
On ev'ry day you meete him through the yeare,
For's bootes and spurs, a horse-man doth appeare.
Was met with, by an odde conceited stranger,
Who friendly told him that he walk'd in danger.
For Sir (in kindenes no way to offend you)
There is a warrant foorth to apprehend you.
Th'offence they say, you riding through thee streete,
Have kil'd a Childe, under your Horses feete.
Sir I protest (quoth he) they doe me wrong,
I have not back'd a horse, God knows how long,
What slaves be these, they have me false bely'd?
Ile proove this twelve-month I did never ride.

Epigram.

What feather'd fowle is this that doth approach
As if it were an *Estredge* in a Coach?
Three yards of feather round about her hat,
And in her hand a bable like to that:
As full of Birdes attire, as Owle, or Goose,
And like unto her gowne, her selfe seemes loose.
Cri'ye mercie Ladie, lewdnes are you there?
Light feather'd stuffe befits you best to weare.

A deafe eare, in a just cause.

A Poore man came unto a Judge & shew'd his wronged
      state,
Entreating him for Jesus sake to be compassionate,
The wrōgs were great he did sustaine, he had no help at al
The Judge sat stil as if the man had spoken to the wall.
With that came two rude fellows in, to have a matter tride
About an Asse, that one had let the other for to ride:
Which Asse the owner found in field, as he by chance past
      by,
And he that hired him a sleepe did in the shadow lye.
For which he would be satisfied, his beast was but to ride:
And for the shadow of his Asse, he would be paid beside.
Great raging words, and damned othes, these two asse-
      wrangles swore,
Whē presently the Judge start up, that seem'd a sleep before
And heard yᵉ follies willingly of these two sottish men,
But bad the poore man come againe, he had no leasure thē.

Epigram.

A Jolly fellow Essex borne and bred,
A Farmers Sonne, his Father being dead,
T'expell his griefe and melancholly passions,
Had vowd himselfe to travell and see fashions.
His great mindes object was no trifling toy,
But to put downe the wandring Prince of Troy.
Londons discoverie first he doth decide,
His man must be his Pilot and his guide.
Three miles he had not past, there he must sit:
He ask't if he were not neere London yet?
His man replies good Sir your selfe besturre,
For we have yet to goe six times as farre.
Alas I had rather stay at home and digge,
I had not thought the worlde was halfe so bigge.
Thus this great worthie comes backe (thoewith strife)
He never was so farre in all his life.
None of the seaven worthies: on his behalfe,
Say, was not he a worthie Essex Calfe?

20

The Humors that haunt a Wife.

A Gentleman a verie friend of mine,
Hath a young wife and she is monstrous fine,
Shee's of the new fantastique humor right,
In her attire an angell of the light.
Is she an Angell? I: it may be well,
Not of the light, she is a light Angell.
Forsooth his doore must suffer alteration,
To entertaine her mightie huge Bom-fashion,
A hood's to base, a hat which she doth male,
With bravest feathers in the Estridge tayle.
She scornes to treade our former proud wives traces.
That put their glory in their on faire faces,
In her conceit it is not faire enough,
She must reforme it with her painters stuffe,
And she is never merry at the heart,
Till she be got into her leatherne Cart.
Some halfe amile the Coach-man guides the raynes,
Then home againe, birladie she takes paines.
My friend seeing what humours haunt a wife,
If he were loose would lead a single life.

A poore Mans pollicy.

Next I will tell you of a poore mans tricke,
Which he did practise with a polliticke,
This poore man had a Cow twas all his stocke,
Which on the Commons fed: where Catell flocke,
The other had a steere a wanton Beast,
Which he did turne to feede amongst the rest.
Which in processe although I know not how,
The rich mans Oxe did gore the poore mans Cow.
The poore man heereat vexed waxed sad,
For it is all the living that he had,
And he must loose his living for a song,
Alas he knew not how to right his wrong.
He knew his enemie had pointes of law,
To save his purse, fill his devouring mawe,
Yet thought the poore man how so it betide,
Ile make him give right sentence on my side.
Without delay unto the Man he goes,
And unto him this fayned tale doth gloze,
(Quoth he) my Cow which with your Oxe did feede,
Hath kild your Oxe and I make knowne the deede.
Why (quoth my Politique) thou shouldst have helpt it
        rather,
Thou shalt pay for him if thow wert my father.
The course of law in no wise must be stayde,
Least I an evill president be made.
O Sir (quoth he) I cry you mercy now,
I did mistake, your Oxe hath gorde my Cow:
Convict by reason he began to brawle,
But was content to let his action fall.
As why? (quoth he) thou lookst unto her well,
Could I prevent the mischiefe that befell?

I have more weightie causes now to trie,
Might orecomes right without a reason why.

Epigram.

One of the damned crew that lives by drinke,
And by Tobacco's stillified stink,
Met with a Country man that dwelt at Hull:
Thought he this pesant's fit to be my Gull.
His first salute like to the French-mans wipe,
Wordes of encounter, please you take a pipe?
The Countrie man amazed at this rabble,
Knewe not his minde yet would be conformable.
Well, in a petty Ale-house they ensconce
His Gull must learne to drinke Tobacco once.
Indeede his purpose was to make a jest,
How with Tobacco he the peasant drest.
Hee takes a whiffe, with arte into his head,
The other standeth still astonished.
Till all his sences he doth backe revoake,
Sees it ascend much like Saint Katherins smoake.
But this indeede made him the more admire,
He saw the smoke: thought he his head's a fier,
And to increase his feare he thought poore soule,
His scarlet nose had been a firie cole.
Which circled round with smoak, seemed to him
Like to some rotten brand that burneth dim.
But to shew wisdome in a desperat case,
He threw a Can of beere into his face,
And like a man some furie did inspire,
Ran out of doores for helpe to quench the fire.
The Ruffin throwes away his Trinidado,
Out comes huge oathes and then his short poynado,
But then the Beere so troubled his eyes,
The countrieman was gone ere he could rise,
A fier to drie him, he doth now require,

Rather than water for to quench his fire.

Epigram.

Come my brave gallant come, uncase, uncase,
Nere shall oblivion your great actes deface.
He has been there where never man came yet,
An unknowne countrie, I, ile warrant it,
Whence he could Ballace a good ship in holde,
With Rubies, Saphiers, Diamonds and golde,
Great Orient Pearles esteem'd no more then moates,
Sould by the pecke as chandlers mesure oates,
I mervaile then we have no trade from thence:
O tis too farre it will not beare expence.
T'were far indeede, a good way from our mayne,
If charges eate up such excessive gaine,
Well he can shew you some of Lybian gravell,
O that there were another world to travell,
I heard him sweare that hee (twas in his mirth)
Had been in all the corners of the earth.
Let all his wonders be together stitcht,
He threw the barre that great *Alcides* pitcht:
But he that saw the Oceans farthest strands,
You pose him if you aske where Dover stands.
He has been under ground and hell did see,
Aeneas nere durst goe so farre as hee.
For he has gone through *Plutœs* Regiment,
Saw how the Fiendes doe Lyers there torment.
And how they did in helles damnation frye,
But who would thinke the Traveller would lye?
To dine with *Pluto* he was made to tarrie,
As kindly us'd as at his Ordinarie.
Hogsheades of wine drawne out into a Tub,
Where he did drinke hand-smooth with *Belzebub*,
And *Proserpine* gave him a goulden bow,

Tis in his chest he cannot shew it now.

Of one that cousned the Cut-purse.

One toulde a Drover that beleev'd it not,
What booties at the playes the Cut-purse got,
But if t'were so my Drovers wit was quicke,
He vow'd to serve the Cut-purse a new tricke.
Next day unto the play, pollicy hy'd,
A bag of fortie shillings by his side,
Which houlding fast he taketh up his stand,
If stringes be cut his purse is in his hand.
A fine conceited Cut-purse spying this,
Lookt for no more, the for shillings his,
Whilst my fine Politique gazed about,
The Cut-purse feately tooke the bottom out.
And cuts the strings, good foole goe make a jest,
This Dismall day thy purse was fairely blest.
Houlde fast good Noddy tis good to dreade the worse,
Your monie's gone, I pray you keepe your purse.
The play is done and foorth the foole doth goe,
Being glad that he cousned the Cut-purse soe.
He thought to jybe how he the Cut-purse drest,
And memorize it for a famous jest.
But putting in his hand it ran quite throw
Dash't the conceite, heele never speake on't now,
You that to playes have such delight to goe,
The Cut-purse cares not, still deceive him so.

29

A drunken fray.

Dicke met with Tom in faith it was their lot,
Two honest Drunkars must goe drinke a pot,
Twas but a pot, or say a little more,
Or say a pot that's filled eight times ore.
But being drunke, and met well with the leese,
They drinke to healthes devoutly on their knees,
Dicke drinks to Hall, to pledge him Tom rejects,
And scornes to doe it for some odde respects
Wilt thou not pledge him thar't a gill, a Scab,
Wert with my man-hood thou deservest a stab,
But tis no matter drinke another bout,
Weele intot'h field and there weele trie it out.
Lets goe (saies Tom) no longer by this hand,
Nay stay (quoth Dicke) lets see if we can stand.
Then forth they goe after the drunken pace,
Which God he knowes was with a reeling grace,
Tom made his bargaine, thus with bonnie Dicke
If it should chance my foote or so should slip,
How wouldst thou use me or after what Size,
Wouldst bare me shorter or wouldst let me rise.
Nay God forbid our quarrells not so great,
To kill thee on advantage in my heat.
Tush we'le not fight for any hate or soe,
But for meere love that each to other owe.
And for thy learning loe Ile shew a tricke,
No sooner spoke the worde but downe comes Dicke,
Well now (quoth Tom) thy life hangs on my sworde,
If I were downe how wouldst thou keepe thy worde?
Why with these hilts I'de braine thee at a blow,
Faith in my humor cut thy throate, or soe,
But Tom he scorne to kill his conquered foe,

Lets Dicke arise, and too't againe they goe.
Dicke throwes downe Tom, or rather Tom did fall,
My hilts (quoth Dicke) shall braine thee like a maull,
Is't so (quoth Tom) good faith what remedie,
The Tower of Babell's fallen and so am I.
But Dicke proceedes to give the fatall wound,
It mist his throate, but run into the ground.
But he supposing that the man was slaine,
Straight fled his contrie, ship himselfe for Spaine,
Whilst valiant Thomas dyed dronken deepe,
Forgot his danger and fell fast a sleepe.

Epigram.

What's he that stares as if he were afright?
The fellowe sure hath seene some dreadfull spright
Masse rightly guest, why sure I did divine,
Hee's haunted with a Spirit feminine.
In plaine termes thus, the Spirit that I meane,
His martiall wife that notable curst queane,
No other weapons but her nailes or fist,
Poore patient Idiot he dares not resist,
His neighbor once would borrow but his knife,
Good neighbor stay (quoth he) ile aske my wife:
Once came he home inspired in the head,
He found his neighbor and his wife a bed,
Yet durst not sturre, but hide him in a hole,
He feared to displease his wife poore soule.
But why should he so dreade and feare her hate,
Since she had given him armor for his pate?
Next day forsooth he doth his neighbor meete,
Whome with sterne rage thus furiously doth greete,
Villaine ile slit thy nose, out comes his knife,
Sirra (quoth he) goe to Ile tell your wife.
Apaled at which terror, meekely faide
Retire good knife my furie is allaide.

Proteus.

Time serving humour thou wrie-faced Ape,
That canst transforme thy selfe to any shape:
Come good *Proteus* come away a pace,
We long to see thy mumping Antique face.
This is the fellow that lives by his wit,
A cogging knave and fawning Parrasit,
He has behaviour for the greatest porte,
And hee has humors for the rascall sorte,
He has beene great with Lordes and high estates,
They could not live without his rare conceites,
He was associat for the bravest spirits,
His galland carriage such favour merrits.
Yet to a Ruffiin humor for the stewes,
A right graund Captaine of the damned crewes,
With whome his humor alwayes is unstable
Mad, melancholly, drunke and variable.
Hat without band like cutting Dicke he goe's,
Renowned for his new invented oathes.
Sometimes like a Civilian, tis strange
At twelve a clocke he must unto the Change,
Where being thought a Marchant to the eye,
He tels strange newes his humor is to lie.
Some Damaske coate the effect thereof must heare,
Invites him home and there he gets good cheare.
But how is't now such brave renowned wits,
Weare ragged robes with such huge gastly slits,
Faith thus a ragged humour he hath got
Whole garments for the Summer are too hot.
Thus you may censure gently if you please,
He weares such garments onely for his ease.
Or thus his credit will no longer wave.

For all men know him for a prating knave.

Epigram.

A Scholer newly entred marriage life
Following his studdie did offend his wife,
Because when she his company expected,
By bookish busines she was still neglected:
Comming unto his studdy, Lord (quoth she)
Can papers cause you love them more than mee:
I would I were transform'd into a Booke
That your affection might upon me looke,
But in my wish, withall be it decreed,
I would be such a Booke you love to reede,
Husband (quoth she) which books form should I take,
Marry (said hee) t'were best an Almanacke,
The reason wherefore I doe wish thee so,
Is, every yeare wee have a new you knowe.

Epigram.

Sira, come hether boy, take view of mee,
My Lady I am purpos'd to goe see:
What doth my feather flourish with a grace,
And this same dooble sette become my face,
How descent doth this doublets forme appeare
(I would I had my sute in houns-ditch heere)
Do not my spurs pronounce a silver sounde?
Do's not my hose circumference profounde?
Sir these are well, but there is one thing ill,
Your Tailour with a sheete of paper bill,
Vowes heel'e be paid, and Serjeants he had feed,
Which wayte your comming forth to do thy deede:
Boy god-amercy let my Lady stay,
Ile see no counter for her sake to day.

Much a doe about chusing a wife.

A Widdower would have a wife were old,
Past charge of children to prevent expence
Her chests and bagges cram'd till they crake with gold,
And she unto her grave post quickly hence,
But if all this were fitting to his minde,
Where is his lease of life to stay behinde?

A Batcheler would have wife were wise,
Faire, Rich and Younge, a maiden for his bed,
Not proude, nor churlish but of fautles size,
A country housewife, in the Citty bred.
But hees a foole and longe in vaine hath staide,
He shoulde bespeake her, there's none ready made.

The taming of a wilde Youth.

Of late a deare and loving friend of mine,
That all his time a Gallant youth had bene,
From mirth to melancholy did decline,
Looking exeeding pale, leane, poore, and thin,
I ask'd the cause he brought me through the streete,
Unto his house, and there hee let me see,
A woman proper, faire, wise and discreete
And said behould, heer's that hath tamed mee,
Hath this (quoth I,) can such a wife do so?
Lord how is he tam'd then, that hath a shrow.

A straunge sighted Traveller.

An honest Country foole being gentle bred,
Was by an odde conceited humor led,
To travell and some English fashions see,
With such strange sights as heere at London be.
Stuffing his purse with a good golden some,
This wandring knight did to the Cittie come,
And there a servingman he entertaines,
An honester in Newgate not remaines.
He shew'd his Maister sights to him most strange,
Great tall Pauls Steeple and the royall-Exchange:
The Bosse at *Billings-gate* and *London-stone*
And at *White-Hall* the monstrous great Whales bone,
Brought him to the banck-side where Beares do dwell
And unto *Shor-ditch* where the whores keepe hell,
Shew'd him the Lyons, Gyants in Guild-Hall,
King *Lud* at *Lud-gate*, the *Babounes* and all,
At length his man, on all he had did pray,
Shew'd him a theevish trick and ran away,
The Traveller turnd home exceeding civill,
And swore in London he had seene the Devill.

Three kinde of Couckoldes,
One, And None.

First there's a Cuckolde called One and None,
Which foole, from fortune hath receiv'd such favour
He hath a wife for beutie stands alone,
Grac'd with good carriage, and most sweete behaviour
Nature so bounteous hath her gifts extended.
From head to foote ther's nothing to be mended.

Besides, she is as perfect chast, as faire,
But being married to a jealous asse,
He vowes she hornes him, for he feeles a paire
Have bin a growing ever since last grasse,
No contrary perswasions hee'l indure,
But's wife is faire and hee's a Cuckolde sure.

The second.
None, and One.

The second hath a wife that loves the game,
And playes the secret cunnig whore at plaisure.
But in her husbands sight shees wondrous tame,
Which makes him vow, he hath *Ulisses* treasure.
Sheele wish al whores were hang'd, with weeping teares
Yet she her selfe a whores cloathes dayly weares.

Her husbāds friends report how's wife doth gull him
With false deceitfull and dissembling showe
And that by both his hornes a man may pull him,
To such a goodly length they daylie growe,
He sayes they wrong her, and he sweares they lye,
His wife is chaste, and in that minde hee'le dye.

The Third,
One, and One.

The third is he that knowes women are weake,
And therefore they are dayly apt to fall,
Words of unkindnesse their kind hearts may breake,
They are but flesh and therefore sinners all,
His wife is not the first hath trod a wry,
Amongst his neighbours he as bad can spye.

What can he helpe it if his wife do ill,
But take it as his crosse and be content,
For quietnesse he lets her have her will,
When shee is old perhaps she will repent,
Let every one amend their one bad life,
Th'are knaves and queans that medle with his wife.

FINIS.